Ryan McCormick

Farts Have Feelings Too

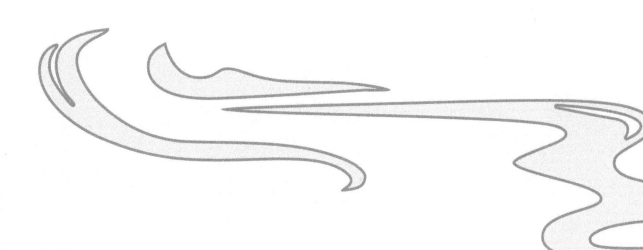

Archway Publishing books may be ordered through booksellers or by contacting:

Archway Publishing
1663 Liberty Drive
Bloomington, IN 47403
www.archwaypublishing.com
844-669-3957

ISBN: 978-1-4808-9744-1 (sc)
ISBN: 978-1-4808-9742-7 (hc)
ISBN: 978-1-4808-9743-4 (e)

Print information available on the last page.

Archway Publishing rev. date: 11/11/2020

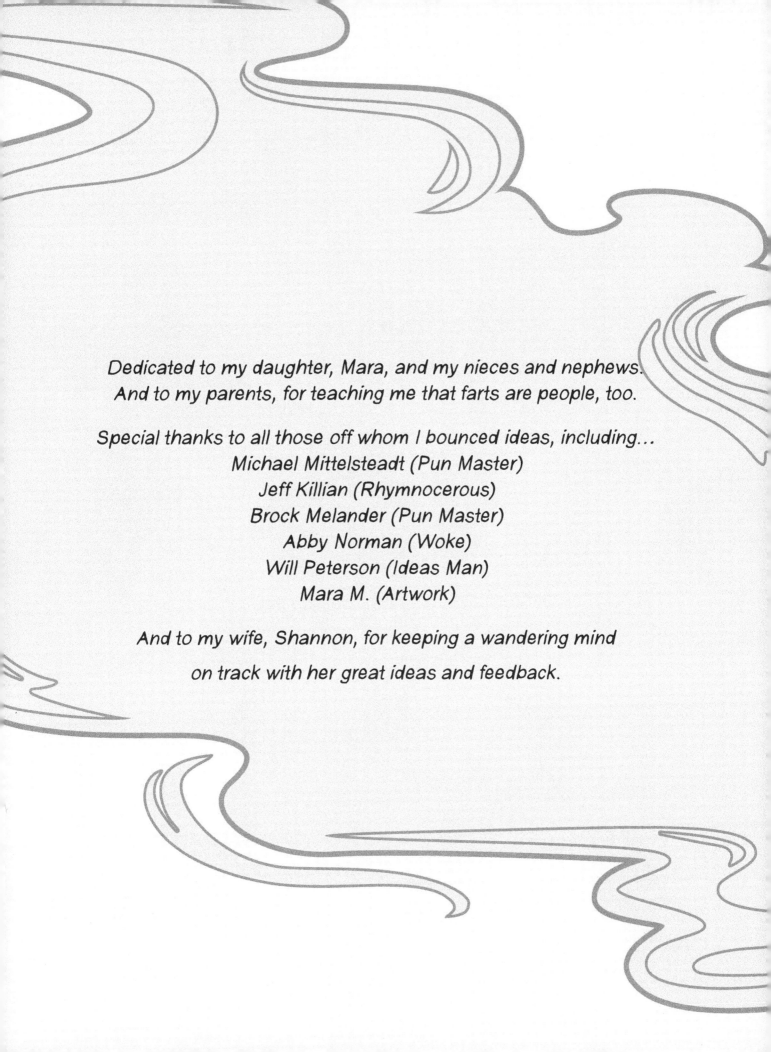

Dedicated to my daughter, Mara, and my nieces and nephews.
And to my parents, for teaching me that farts are people, too.

Special thanks to all those off whom I bounced ideas, including...
Michael Mittelsteadt (Pun Master)
Jeff Killian (Rhymnocerous)
Brock Melander (Pun Master)
Abby Norman (Woke)
Will Peterson (Ideas Man)
Mara M. (Artwork)

And to my wife, Shannon, for keeping a wandering mind

on track with her great ideas and feedback.

Farts are funny because someone toots, and it's funny because it's really from your butt—we don't know why.
                                        —Rori N., age five

Some call them farts; some call them toots.
Sometimes they slip when your butt scoots!

They're cheese that's cut; they're wind that's broken.
They tell the world, "The bowels have spoken!"

Across the land, they have many names.
But everywhere, they're treated the same.

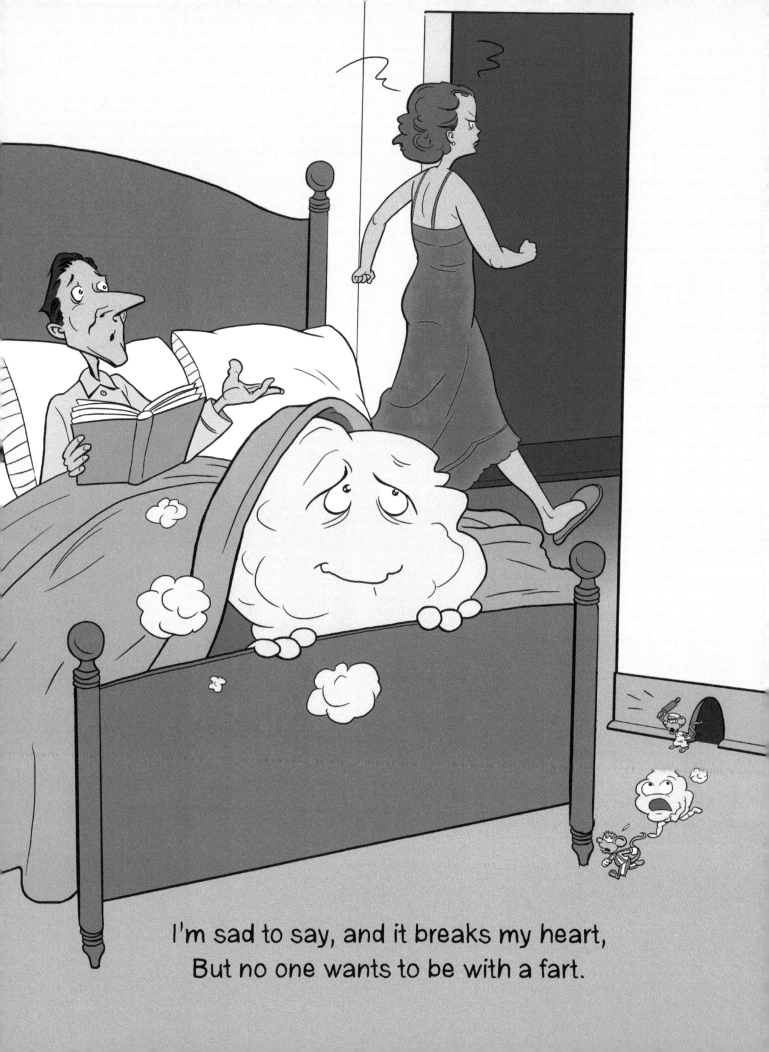

I'm sad to say, and it breaks my heart,
But no one wants to be with a fart.

No one waves when they pass gas.
We hide our farts as if they're trash.

No one claims a fart that's theirs.
How we treat farts is so unfair!

Farts are social; they love to party!
(A spicy dish makes *everyone* farty.)

But when farts get caught, as they often do,
They get kicked out with a spray or two.

So into the night the farts slink away,
Hoping tomorrow is a better day.

They smell a bit; I admit that's true.
But remember—farts have feelings too!

Farts should be our closest friends.
We make them from our own rear ends!

Who knows which types of fart they'll be?
They're gassy, risky mysteries!

Farts come to us when we're unwell.
It's soothing, their familiar smell.

When winter comes and cold's the norm,
Farts know how to keep us warm.

Even dogs enjoy a fart,
Thinking it's a work of art.

Grandpas, too, may like a toot.
At ninety-nine they're still a hoot!

When we want our friends to linger,
Here's a game: "Pull my finger!"

And when we want to be alone,
Farts can say, "Time to go home!

Farts bring us joy and make us smile,
But only last a little while.

So love your farts as they love you,
And know that farts have feelings too!

THE END

CPSIA information can be obtained
at www.ICGtesting.com
Printed in the USA
LVHW012122211220
674786LV00006B/326

9 781480 897441